Fingerplays and Action Chants

Volume Two:

Family and Friends

Fingerplays and Action Chants

Volume Two:
Family and Friends

By
Tonja Evetts Weimer

PEARCE-EVETTS PUBLISHING

Pittsburgh, Pennsylvania

This book and audio cassette contain fingerplays and chants about family and friends for children ages two to eight. The book is designed primarily for parents and teachers, but can be used by children. It contains hand motions and actions to do with the songs on the cassette and additional teacher resources.

**Fingerplays and Action Chants
Volume Two: Family and Friends**

By Tonja Evetts Weimer

Published by:
Pearce Evetts Publishing
P.O. Box 79117
Pittsburgh, PA 15216, U.S.A.
(412) 344-5451

Weimer, Tonja Evetts
    Fingerplays and action chants, volume II: family and friends/Tonja Evetts Weimer.
    Includes bibliographical references
    Library of Congress Catalog Card Number: 94-073897
    ISBN 0-936823-14-3

Dedicated to Kenny, Alli, Malini and Aneysha

CONTENTS

ACKNOWLEDGMENTS

The success and completion of any project always seems to be due to a team effort, and to how well that team can work in harmony and in support of one another. That was certainly so in the formation of *Fingerplays and Action Chants, Volumes One and Two*.

Heading the team in coordinating everyone's efforts and producing both books was my husband, Vik Pearce. His vision for both books was both artistic and practical, and his organizational skills were essential in bringing them to press.

In the art department, we thank Yvonne Kozlina for an inspirational job of capturing the feeling of the rhymes in her original work. Whether the feeling be surprise, humor, suspense or concentration, we could see it in her pictures as we spoke the words to the rhymes.

INTRODUCTION

Fingerplays and chants are fun for children, as well as being effective teaching tools. Because they are rhythmical and contain surprise or humor, children listen to them more closely and sharpen their listening skills.

With this improvement in listening skills comes language learning. The imitative process of learning these fingerplays teaches voice inflection and volume, pronunciation, enunciation, vocabulary, and phrasing. In many of the fingerplays there is a sequence of events and frequently a suspenseful build-up. Both of these qualities make them easy and fun for young children to dramatize. The rhythm and rhyme are also infectious, inviting children to action and movement.

Other values of fingerplays and chants include the teaching of colors and numbers and other general learning concepts in a simple, unstructured way. They can also help make transitions from one activity to another flow more smoothly, or just change the pace in a day's activities.

These fingerplays can be enjoyed by children of all ages, but they are selected especially for those from the ages of two to six years old. They are all favorites of mine, tried and proven with children in classrooms and with adults in workshops. They also work especially well with children of all ages in special education classes.

HOW TO USE FINGERPLAYS AND CHANTS

Fingerplays and chants can be used for a specified activity period, or they can be sprinkled throughout the day. We see them used most often during "circle time" or "group time" in early childhood settings. (This group time may involve the entire class or it may be a small group as a part of the class.) Group times last anywhere from ten minutes (roll call, greeting, etc.) to half an hour (music, story time, conversation, etc.). Whenever children have been sitting for any period of time, they need a break from listening. Fingerplays and chants teach, as well as provide that needed change of pace.

Good classroom management requires a balancing of activities from quiet, to active, to semi-active. Just as children cannot sit quietly for too long, neither can they engage in full physical movement for too long without tiring. Fingerplays and chants can provide a restful pause, calm, soothe and bring children back to attention. I have often used the action chant, "Teddy Bear, Teddy Bear," as a transition to lead children back to a quiet place to work. Children get caught up in doing the chant and then automatically follow the instructions at the end that say, "Teddy Bear, Teddy Bear, sit down please." With that line, you have their full attention, and you can quietly and calmly tell them what their next activity is. This is so much more simple — so much more positive — than shouting at noisy children to go back to their seats, to be quiet, or to sit down. Smoothly and effortlessly, children can be returned to calm and purposeful activity.

All units of study in the early childhood curriculum are enhanced with a poem, song, rhyme or chant. Volume Two, Family and Friends, speaks to all children universally and the collection in this book will enrich the child's personal experience of people and relationships. Children remember each rhyme more easily if they have also had a chance to act it out or dramatize it.

At home, parents can use fingerplays and chants anytime during the day and especially before bedtime. These fun-filled rhymes lend themselves easily to the intimate bonding process between parent and child — the quiet time of laughing, talking, listening and cuddling. Children will repeat the rhymes long after the parent has taught it to them, and remember those warm moments when they shared them together.

Finally, this book contains two action chants that work so wonderfully with children that they need special mention.

"My Mama Told Me" is an action chant I collected from the American South that can be adapted for use as a fingerplay, for simple body movement, or for full body movement. When it is used as a fingerplay, children can sit and snap their fingers, wave hello, wiggle their thumbs, brush their palms, and any other action that involves the hands. Simple body movement would involve non-locomotor activities such as wiggling the nose, winking an eye, tapping toes, patting the head, and other non-locomotor actions. Full body movement would include locomotor skills such as walking, jumping, turning, rolling, etc.

To demonstrate the versatility of this fingerplay, "My Mama Told Me" (Version One) opens side one of the cassette accompanying this book. It has the children perform simple actions and then moves them to a standing position. The rest of the rhymes can be done either standing or sitting. "My Mama Told Me" (*Version Two*) concludes side one of the cassette and has the children do some more simple actions and then moves them back to a sitting position. Thus, the sequence of activity is brought from beginning to end.

Side two of the cassette begins and ends with "One, Two, What Shall We Do?", another versatile action chant that serves a similar purpose in starting and concluding the next set of activities. That is why we use both of these chants twice in this book.

And the best use of all of these memorable chants is for you and your children to make up your own sequence of actions -- and to have fun!!

MY MAMA TOLD ME
Version One

This chant is a gem. First, the rhythm is infectious and one not likely to be forgotten. Second, it has great flexibility, and adults and children can make up the actions however they choose. It also continues to be one of my favorite chants for leading children from one activity to another.

The rhythm of this chant is all important for it to be effective. Be sure to put the emphasis on the words in bold type: **ME**, **YOU**, and **I**.

My mama told **ME**

To tell **YOU**

To clap your hands like **I** do!

Repeat verse for the following actions:

Nod your head

Snap your fingers

Stand up straight

Tap your toes

Bend your knees

Wave hello

WHO STOLE THE COOKIE?

"Who Stole the Cookie?" is a clapping chant that can be done alone, or with a partner. The children can count as high as they want to go.

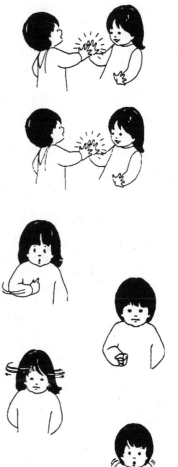

Who stole the cookie from
    the cookie jar?

Number one stole the cookie
    from the cookie jar.

*(Two children clap hands together
    on these two phrases)*

Who me?

Yes, you.

Couldn't be!

Then who?

(Repeat sequence at least up to number 5.)

MOTHER'S KNIVES AND FORKS

"Mother's Knives and Forks" has been enjoyed by very young children for many years. Its brevity and simple actions make it easy to remember.

These are mother's knives and forks,

This is mother's table,

(Palms downward)

This is mother's looking glass,
(Palms inward)

And this is the baby's cradle.
(Rock)

(For the tune to this rhyme, listen to the cassette, which sings it three times. The last time it is sung softly.)

THIS IS MOTHER

This is a simple rhyme for the very young, using all five fingers on one hand. If your child's family does not "match" the one being described here, always feel free to improvise, changing the characters to fit the family in his or her life.

This is mother,

This is father,

This is brother tall.

This is sister,

This is baby,
    smallest one of all.

(Repeat on the other hand)

An example of changing the rhyme to suit an individual child is, "This is mother, this is grandma, this is uncle tall. This is cousin, this is baby, smallest one of all." This rhyme could be the catalyst to a full discussion about what a family is.

THIS IS THE WAY THE LADIES RIDE

This nursery rhyme can be said in unison, like all others, or it can be done with a child bouncing on an adult's knee to the rhythm of the words. It is an excellent speech and language game, as the child watches the adult pronounce the words, hears them, and feels their rhythm, all at the same time.

Another way to use this chant is to have children gallop around the room to the rhythm of the words.

This is the way the ladies ride:
    Tri-tree, Tri-tree, Tri-tree,
      Tri-Tree.

(Bounce gently)

This is the way the gentlemen ride:
    Gallop-a-trot, Gallop-a-trot,
      Gallop-a-trot.

(Bounce a little more)

And this is the way the farmers ride:
    Hobble-dee-hoy, Hobble-dee-hoy,
      Hobble-dee-hoy.

(Bounce high)

THERE WERE FIVE IN THE BED

This rhyme can be sung or said, done on the fingers, or fully dramatized. Its versatility makes it a favorite, and, through repeated use, children learn to count. Some children like to say it as "10 In the Bed" which is great for counting purposes as long as the children don't get silly from having too much repetition.

There were five in the bed
And the little one said,

"Roll over, roll over."

So they all rolled over

And one fell out.

(Repeat, counting backward with 4, then 3, 2, 1, until there are none in the bed)

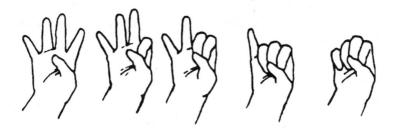

Last verse:

There were none in the bed
And the little one said,

"Goodnight.

Sleep tight."

HERE'S A BALL

"Here's A Ball" is fun for very young children. The actions are easy for little hands and arms, it teaches counting to three, and it's short and simple to remember.

Here's a ball.

Here's a ball.

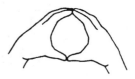

And a great BIG ball I see.

Can you count them?
Are you ready?

One.

Two.

Three!

MY MAMA TOLD ME
Version Two

This version completes the cycle of activity started in *Version One* and brings the children back to a sitting position.

My mama told **ME**

To tell **YOU**

To clap your hands like, **I** do!

Other Activities:

Shake your hands

Bend your knees

Turn around

Reach up high

Sit back down

Wave goodbye

ONE, TWO, WHAT SHALL WE DO?
Version One

"One, Two, What Shall We Do?" is an action chant that teaches counting to ten and is excellent for leading children from quiet to active experiences, or vice versa.

It is used twice in this book, to accompany the activities on the cassette. In *Version One*, children are brought to a standing position.

One, two,
    what shall we do?

Three, four,
    stand up once more.

Five, six,
    my arms and legs I'll fix.

Seven, eight,
    I'm standing up straight.

Nine, ten,
    I'm looking and listening again.

WAY UP IN AN APPLE TREE

"Way Up In An Apple Tree" is not only fun to say, but also to dramatize. Children truly enjoy "shaking" the tree to get the fruit down. You can substitute other fruit trees, and thus, count as high as you want.

Way up in an apple tree,

One little apple smiled

Down at me.

I shook that tree as hard
    as I could.

Down came the apple.

Hmmmmmm, it was good.

Other verses:

Two oranges; Three pears; Four plums; Five peaches

(Example: Way up in an orange tree, two little oranges smiled down at me, etc.)

HEAD-ACHER, EYE-WINKER

This is an old nursery rhyme favorite, which is short, fun, and probably remembered by many adults whose parents taught it to them. Parents can use this one before the children go to sleep. Teachers can use it with each nursery school child before they leave for the day, as a way to connect with each one personally. Rhymes and games such as this let us play with children individually and help to remind us to be sure that we have given special attention to each child every day.

Head-acher

Eye-winker

Nose-smeller

Mouth-eater

Chin-chopper, chin-chopper
  chin-chopper, chin

Gilley, gilley, gilley, gilley.
(Tickle under the chin)

THIS IS THE CHURCH

This is another old standard. Children enjoy practicing the finger motions over and over as they repeat the words. This rhyme can also be sung.

This is the church,

This is the steeple,

Open the doors,

And see all the people.
(Turn palms and fingers up.)

(Use the cassette to hear the tune. The cassette sings this rhyme twice.)

FIVE LITTLE SOLDIERS

This rhyme counts forward to five and possesses humor and surprise for young children.

One, two, three, four, five!

Five little soldiers
     standing in a row.

Three stood tall,
     but two stood so.

Up walked the sergeant,
     and what do you think?

Up popped the soldiers,
     as quick as a wink!

(This fingerplay repeats on the cassette)

WHERE IS THUMBKIN?

This is a singing fingerplay for the very young, and one they never seem to tire of.

Where is **Thumbkin**? Where
is **Thumbkin**?

Here I am!
(*One arm to the front*)

Here I am!
(*Other arm to the front*)

How are you today, sir?

Very well, I thank you.

Run away.
(*One arm behind back*)

Run away.
(*Other arm behind back*)

*(Replace **Thumbkin** with other fingers:*
    2-Pointer, 3-Tall Man, 4-Ring Man,
    5-Baby)

*(Last verse: Replace "Where is **Thumbkin**?" with "Where are all the men?" and "Here I am!" with "Here we are!")*

"Where is Thumbkin?" can be used as a fingerplay, as shown here, or as a "call and response" singing game. Substitute a child's name for Thumbkin. Example:

    Teacher: Where is Mary? Where is Mary?
    Child: Here I am! Here I am!
    Teacher: How are you today, miss?
    Child: Very well, I thank you.
    Teacher: Sit back down.

(Or, sing what you want the child to do, i.e., stand up straight; go get your coat; get in line; go outside; or whatever instruction you want to give.)

Used in this way, "Where Is Thumbkin?" can be a language assessment guide as well as a great transition tool.

ONE, TWO, WHAT SHALL WE DO?
Version Two

This version has the children sit back down, and brings all of the activities to completion.

One, two,
   what shall we do?

Three, four,
   sit down once more.

Five, six,
   my arms and legs I'll fix.
(Cross arms and legs)

Seven, eight,
   I'm sitting up straight.

Nine, ten,
   I'm looking and listening again.

Bibliography

BIBLIOGRAPHY

Animal Books

Ahlberg, Allen and Janet. *The Jolly Postman or Other People's Letters*. Boston: Little Brown & Co., 1986.

Asch, Frank. *Moonbear Loves the Moon*. New York: Simon & Schuster 1993.

Bemelmans, Ludwig. *Madeline, A Pop-Up Book*. Viking Penguin, 1987.

Caldwell, Mary. *Morning, Rabbit, Morning*. Illustrated by Ann Schweninger. New York: Harper & Row, Publishers, 1982.

Campbell, Rod. *Oh Dear!* London: Blackie and Son Furnival House Ltd., 1983.

Carle, Eric. *The Honeybee and the Robber*. New York: Putnam, 1981.

Carter, David. *How Many Bugs in a Box?* New York: Simon & Schuster,1988.

_____. *More Bugs in Boxes*. New York: Simon & Schuster, 1990.

Cremins, Robert, designer and illustrator. *My Animal ABC's*. New York: Crown, 1983.

Crowther, Robert. *The Most Amazing Hide-and-Seek Counting Book*. New York: Viking, 1981.

Demi. *The Little Elephants*. New York: Random House, 1981.

_____. *Where is Willie Worm?* New York: Random House, 1981.

Faulkner, Keith. *Oh No!* New York: Simon & Schuster Books for Young Readers, 1992.

Fowler, Richard. *Squirrel's Tale*. Tulsa, Oklahoma: Educational Development Corporation, 1983.

_____. Richard. *There's a Mouse About the House*. Tulsa, Oklahoma: Educational Development Corporation, 1983.

Gurney, Eric. *The Pop-Up Book of Dogs.* New York: Random House.

Hawkins, Colin. *Adding Animals.* New York: Putnam, 1983.

Hill, Eric. *Animals Peek-A-Book.* Price, Stern, Sloan:Los Angeles;1982.

_____. *Spot's Birthday Party.* New York: Putnam, 1982.

_____. *Spot's First Christmas.* New York: Putnam, 1983.

_____. *Spot's First Walk.* New York: Putnam, 1981.

_____. *Where's Spot.* New York: Putnam, 1980.

Hooker, Yvonne. *One Green Frog.* Illustrations by Carlo A. Michelini. New York: Grosset and Dunlap, 1981.

Kraus, Robert. *Whose Mouse Are You?* Illustrations by Jose Aruego. New York: Collier Books, 1970.

Lear, Edward. *The Owl and the Pussycat.* 1993.

Le Sieg, Theo. *The Many Mice of Mr. Brice.* Illustrated by Roy McKie. New York: Random House.

Lustig, Loretta, Illustrator. *The Pop-up Book of the Circus.* New York: Random House, 1979.

Peppe, Rodney. *Run Rabbit, Run!* New York: Delacorte, 1982.

Pienkowski, Jan. *Dinner Time* London: Gallery Five Ltd., 1980.

_____. *Gossip.* Los Angeles: Price, Stern, Sloan, 1982.

_____. *Road Hog.* Los Angeles: Price, Stern, Sloan, 1993.

Tarrant, Graham. *Frogs.* Designed by Douglas Maxwell. Illustrated by Tony King. Published by Natural Pop-Ups.

Walser, David. *My Bear Book.* Los Angeles: Price, Stern, Sloan, 1982.

Zelinsky, Paul. *The Wheels On the Bus.* Santa Monica, California: Intervisual Books, Inc., 1991.

Nursery Rhymes

Cremins, Robert, designer and illustrator. *My Animal Mother Goose.* New York: Crown, 1983.

Hill, Eric. *Nursery Rhymes Peek-A-Book.* Los Angeles: Price, Stern, Sloan,1982.

Korky, Paul. "Humpty Dumpty." *Rhyming Pop-Ups.* New York: Simon and Schuster, 1983.

_____. "Jack and Jill and Other Nursery Rhymes." *The Real Mother Goose Pop-Ups.* Los Angeles: Rand McNally, 1985.

_____. "Jack and Jill." *Rhyming Pop-Ups.* New York: Simon and Schuster, 1983.

_____. "Humpty Dumpty and Other Nursery Rhymes." *The Real Mother Goose Pop-Ups.* Los Angeles: Rand McNally, 1985.

_____. "Jack and Jill." *Rhyming Pop-Ups.* New York: Simon and Schuster, 1983."

_____. "Sing a Song of Sixpence." *Rhyming Pop-Ups.* New York: Simon and Schuster, 1983.

Korky, Paul and Marshall, Ray. "Hey Diddle Diddle." *Rhyming Pop-Ups.* New York: Simon and Schuster, 1983.

Paris, Pat, illustrator, and Dick Dudley, paper engineer. "Humpty Dumpty and Other Nursery Rhymes." *The Real Mother Goose Pop-Ups.* Los Angeles: Rand McNally, 1985.

_____. "The Cat and the Fiddle and Other Nursery Rhymes." *The Real Mother Goose Pop-Ups.* Los Angeles: Rand McNally, 1985.

Paris, Pat. "Pat-a-Cake and Other Nursery Rhymes." *The Real Mother Goose Pop-Ups.* Los Angeles: Rand McNally, 1985.

Pop-Up Mother Goose. New York: Random House, 1978.

The Sesame Street Mother Goose. New York: Random House and
   Children's Television Workshop, 1976.

TEACHER RESOURCES

Folk Records

Jenkins, Ella. *Early Childhood Songs.* New York: Folkways.

Raffi. *Everything Grows.* Ontario, Canada: Troubador Records, Ltd., 1987.

_____. *More Singable Songs.* Ontario, Canada: Troubador Records, Ltd.,
   1977.

_____. *One Light, One Sun.* Ontario, Canada: Troubador Records, Ltd.,
   1990.

_____. *Rise and Shine.* Ontario, Canada: Troubador Records, Ltd., 1982.

_____. *Singable Songs for the Very Young.* Ontario, Canada: Troubador
   Records, Ltd., 1976.

Weimer, Tonja Evetts. *Animal Friends For Sale.* Pittsburgh, Pennsylvania:
   Pearce-Evetts Publishing, 1983.

_____. *Space Songs for Children.* (book and cassette). Pittsburgh,
   Pennsylvania: Pearce-Evetts Publishing, 1993.

_____. *Tonja Evetts Weimer Sings Folksongs for Children.* Pittsburgh,
   Pennsylvania: Pearce-Evetts Publishing, 1983.

Fingerplay Books and Cassettes

Weimer, Tonja Evetts. *Fingerplays and Action Chants, Volume One:
   Animals.* Pittsburgh, Pennsylvania: Pearce-Evetts Publishing, 1995.

_____. *Fingerplays and Action Chants, Volume Two: Family and Friends.*
   Pittsburgh, Pennsylvania: Pearce-Evetts Publishing, 1996.

Songbooks

Amery, Heather. *Children's Songbook.* London: Usborne Publishing, 1988.

Beall, Pamela Conn and Nipp, Susan Hagen. *We Sing.* Los Angeles: Price, Stern,Sloan, 1982.

Bryan, Ashley. *All Night, All Day.* New York: Atheneum, Macmillian, 1991.

Frank, Josette. *Poems to Read to the Very Young.* New York: Random House, 1982.

Fox, Dan and Marks, Claude. *Go In and Out the Window.* New York: Metropolitan Museum of Art, Henry Holt & Co., 1987.

Hart, Jane. *Sing Bee!* New York: Lothrop Lee & Shepard Books Publishing, 1989.

John, Timothy. *The Great Song Book.* New York: Doubleday, 1975.

Krull, Kathleen. *Gonna Sing My Head Off.* New York: Knopf, 1992.

Larrick, Nancy. *Songs from Mother Goose.* New York: Harper & Row, 1989.

ABOUT THE AUTHOR

Tonja Evetts Weimer was born in Bakersfield, California and was raised in a family of cowboys and cattle ranchers. She grew up hearing her father's auctioneering chant and the folk songs of the Oklahomans who fled to California to escape the dust bowl.

One of twenty National Fellows chosen by the U.S. Department of Education, she obtained an M.A in Early Childhood Education at San Francisco State College. Tonja has been a supervisor; director of early childhood programs; owner and director of her own creative dance and music schools; and a national consultant to schools and educational programs.

A recipient of grants from the Pittsburgh Foundation, Alcoa and the Hunt Foundations, Tonja adapted her music and dance program to children of special needs. She was a key presenter at the 1987 Special Olympics at the request of the Kennedy Foundation.

In 1993 Tonja was encouraged to write songs about outer space for young children. The result was a cassette and book *Space Songs for Children*, which won two national awards from the Institute of Childhood Resources and was rated "Top 100 Products for Children 1994" and "Top 10 Audio Products for 1994".

Tonja Weimer has performed in concert for the astronauts and their families at the Johnson Space Center in Houston and at many other NASA sites. She travels throughout the U.S. and in other countries performing "Space Concerts" for thousands of children and training adults in creative ways to teach children through music and movement. She is a frequent keynote speaker at educational conferences and makes regular TV appearances.

Tonja has produced six books, five albums and two videos. She lives in Pittsburgh with her husband, Vik Pearce, and has four children. Her charisma makes her an artist in great demand.

MATERIALS FROM TONJA EVETTS WEIMER

These books, tapes and videos can be obtained through your favorite book store, or ordered from PEP Publishing, P.O. Box 79117, Pittsburgh, PA 15216. Phone orders, have your VISA or Mastercard ready and call 1-800-842-9571. Shipping is 10% with a $3.00 minimum. PA residents add 7% tax. Please use the order form on the last page.

Animals Friends for Sale

This release is full of favorite children's folk songs about animals. You will hear the influence of Tonja's cowboy heritage on this album and experience why children are captivated by her music. This album is rich in creative movement potential.

Cassette: ISBN 0-936823-06-2 $9.95

Creative Dance and Movement

This is a teacher's guide to Tonja's creative dance and movement program. This illustrated book includes philosophy, lesson plans and creative activity details that make it a must for the early childhood classroom.

Book $8.95

Fingerplays and Action Chants, Vol. I: Animals

This includes the very best fingerplays and singing games about animals. These are instantaneous favorites which include the "Bear Hunt." Great for car trips. The illustrated 64 page book has all the fingerplay hand motions and includes teacher resources.

Book and Cassette Set: ISBN 0-936823-13-5 $14.95
Cassette only: ISBN 0-936823-01-1 $8.95

Fingerplays and Action Chants, Vol. II: Family and Friends

These are Tonja's favorite fingerplays and action songs about family and friends. Children love the sound effects on the tape and stay involved for hours. It Includes

"My Mama Told Me," an all time favorite. The illustrated 64 page book has all the fingerplay hand motions and includes teacher resources.

Book and Cassette Set: ISBN 0-936823-14-3 $14.95
Cassette only: ISBN 0-936823-03-8 $8.95

Folksongs for Children

These songs are an instantaneous children's favorite, especially designed for creative movement activities. Sequentially arranged folk favorites provide quiet, semi-active and then active participation in a blend that is Tonja's specialty.

Cassette: ISBN 0-936823-05-04 $9.95

Frolicking Frogs; A Time To Sing And Dance

Folksongs, counting fingerplays and stories about frogs set the mood for children to go into the swamp and dance to "Frog Boogie."

Video: ISBN 0-936823-10-0 $19.95

Rhymes and Rainbows: A Time to Sing And Dance

You'll discover folksongs, including "Jenny Jenkins," fingerplays and a story about rainbows. Children will learn colors as they dance with streamers under the rainbow.

Video: ISBN 0-936823-09-7 $19.95

Space Songs for Children

You'll love how Tonja transforms space into a magical place where children sing and dance and learn science. There are bouncy tunes and action songs to get children moving and there are quiet songs and soft lullabies to soothe children. The 104 page book designed for parents and teachers is full of activities and resources about space.

Book and Cassette Set: ISBN 0-936823-11-9 $14.95
Cassette only: ISBN 0-936823-12-7 $9.95

ORDER FORM

Telephone Orders: Call Toll Free: 1-800-842-9571. Have your Visa or Master Card ready.

FAX Orders to: (412) 571-1217

Postal Order: Mail to PEP Publishing, P.O. Box 79117, Pittsburgh, PA 15216, USA.
(412) 344-5451

PLEASE SEND THE FOLLOWING:

I understand that I may return anything for a full refund for any reason, **no questions asked.**

Item	Price
_____	_____
_____	_____
_____	_____
_____	_____
_____	_____

Shipping: Book Rate: 10% with $3.00 minimum. (Surface shipping may take three to four weeks)
Air Mail: $4.00 per item.

Subtotal _____

PA Residents
ADD 7% TAX _____

Shipping _____

Total _____

o Please send me Tonja's brochure FREE.

Company Name: _____

Name: _____

Address: _____

City: _____ State _____ Zip _____

Telephone: _____

Payments: o Check o Credit Card: o Visa o Mastercard

Card Number: _____

Name on Card: _____ Exp. Date: _____